DINOSAURS

Note: On page 48 there is a list of some dinosaur names and how to say them.

DINOSAURS

By J. B. Wright

Illustrated by Gene Biggs

A GOLDEN BOOK • NEW YORK

Western Publishing Company, Inc., Racine, Wisconsin 53404

Dinosaurs were land reptiles that lived on earth long before people. The first dinosaurs were here about 220 million years ago. They disappeared suddenly about 65 million years ago, and no one is sure why.

Some scientists think that a star exploded
somewhere close to earth, killing off many
creatures. Others think that a huge meteorite hit
the earth and destroyed so many plants that the
dinosaurs starved to death.

Here are some of the dinosaurs you will meet in this book. They could only be seen together on a chart like this because they lived at different times during a period of more than 150 million years—the Age of Dinosaurs.

Compsognathus

Camarasaurus

Plateosaurus

Ankylosaurus

Staurikosaurus

Stegosaurus

Mamenchisaurus

Scutellosaurus

Iguanodon

Tyrannosaurus

Hypsilophodon

Brachiosaurus

Saltasaurus

Triceratops

Allosaurus

Edmontosaurus

Stenonychosaurus

Apatosaurus

Coelurus

Parasaurolophus

Fossil hunters at work

Dinosaurs died out millions of years before
the first human beings lived. How can we be sure
they ever existed?

By studying their *fossils*—the dinosaur bones
and teeth and footprints that have been buried
and preserved in rocks—scientists have found
remains of about one hundred and fifty different
kinds of dinosaurs all over the world.

New and different dinosaurs are still being found. Recently, scientists found a new dinosaur in Arizona. They named it **Scutellosaurus**.

Its tail was longer than the rest of its body, but altogether it was only four feet long. Its head was small, a little like an iguana's is today. It ate plants.

When we think of dinosaurs, we think BIG. In our minds, we picture giant creatures. The truth is that many dinosaurs were very small.

Staurikosaurus, one of the first dinosaurs—it lived 210 million years ago—was about six and a half feet long and had sharp, pointed teeth. Its tail was about half its length. It probably ate meat.

Stenonychosaurus, one of the last dinosaurs on earth, was also small. Found both in Canada and Mongolia, it was six and a half feet long and weighed sixty to one hundred pounds. In relation to its size, it had the largest brain of all the dinosaurs. It was a meat-eater.

brain size

One of the smallest of all dinosaurs was **Compsognathus**. About two and a half feet long, it weighed about six pounds and was not much bigger than a chicken. In fact, it looked a lot like a bird. Found in Germany and France, it ate lizards, insects, and other small creatures.

Big dinosaurs, of course, could be very big. **Brachiosaurus**, whose fossil remains have been found in East Africa as well as in Colorado, grew about as big as they came: seventy-five feet long, weighing 150,000 pounds. Its neck was almost half the length of its body. It walked on four legs and ate plants.

If a full-sized elephant of today could stand beside Brachiosaurus, the dinosaur would be about three times the elephant's height and ten times its weight.

The dinosaurs that ate other animals—the meat-eaters—were often small in size. They could move quickly and were good hunters.

Coelurus had long back legs for running rapidly, and short forelegs with two fingers and a thumb with which it could grab lizards and frogs easily.

Some meat-eating dinosaurs were big. For instance, there was **Allosaurus**, which was thirty-six feet long and weighed from two thousand to four thousand pounds. It had enormous claws on its three-fingered hands and feet. It probably hunted and caught Coelurus for its supper.

Large dinosaurs that ate only plants needed huge bellies to hold and digest all the leafy plants they swallowed.

Camarasaurus was sixty feet long, had a box-shaped head, and walked on all four of its heavy legs. Like other big dinosaurs, it probably swallowed stones to help grind up the food in its stomach.

Hypsilophodon, which has been found in England, Portugal, and the United States, was quite small. No more than seven and a half feet long, it also was a plant-eater. It ate plants that grew close to the ground. It could run fast and hide easily among the leaves of low-growing plants. Hypsilophodons managed to survive for more than 80 million years.

Plateosaurus was an early, long-necked dinosaur. It could stretch to eat leaves growing on tall trees. It could also rear up even higher on its hind legs, using its tail to help it balance.

Millions of years later a strange-looking
dinosaur about the same size as Plateosaurus
ate flowering plants. **Parasaurolophus** had a
curved, hollow crest that grew on top of its skull.
Its nose bones were hollow tubes, and probably it
could make a loud sound, like a trombone,
through these air passages.

During the Age of Dinosaurs, many other animals lived on earth, too. There were lizards, frogs, snails, turtles, crocodiles, birds, and various insects.

There were flying reptiles called pterosaurs
that swooped and glided through the air. There
were swimming reptiles called ichthyosaurs and
plesiosaurs that swam in the oceans. And there
were snakes much like those today.

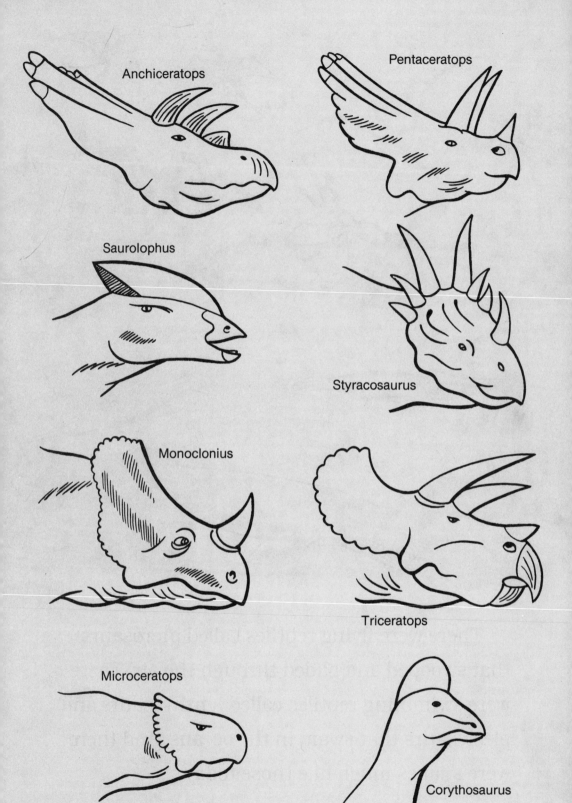

Anchiceratops

Pentaceratops

Saurolophus

Styracosaurus

Monoclonius

Triceratops

Microceratops

Corythosaurus

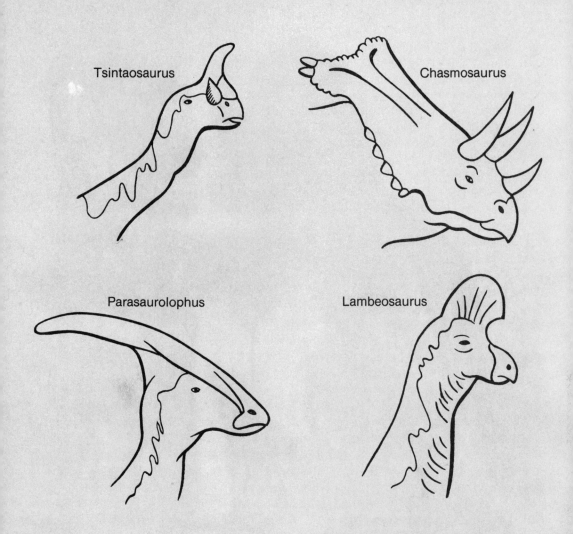

Tsintaosaurus

Chasmosaurus

Parasaurolophus

Lambeosaurus

Look at all these dinosaurs with their strange
crests, horns, flaps, and neck frills made of bone.
Crests might have helped dinosaurs of the
same kind recognize each other. The tubes that
ran through many of the crests may have let
dinosaurs make loud honking sounds. Horns
and frills certainly gave some protection to the
dinosaurs that had them.

23

Saltasaurus, a large dinosaur (forty feet long), had thousands of bony plates covering its body. These provided a kind of armor-plating, protecting this giant creature from its enemies. Like all other known armor-plated dinosaurs, it was a plant-eater.

Ankylosaurus, found both in Canada and in China, was another armor-plated dinosaur. It had bony plates even on its head! Also, its tail ended in a big bony knob. Ankylosaurus could swing it like a club. None of its enemies wanted to be in the way of that powerful weapon.

Stegosaurus had big pointed plates—looking almost like sails—running down its back in two rows. Some scientists say the plates were not strong enough for use as armor. They may have been a cooling device.

Stegosaurus did, however, have a fine weapon—its spiked tail!

Triceratops had strong jaws, sharp teeth, a pincerlike beak, three horns on its head, and a "frill" or collar at the back of its head. Its beak must have been helpful for snapping off the branches of plants.

Dinosaurs were amazing animals. Let's look more closely at their necks, teeth, claws, and skin.

Brachiosaurus

Mamenchisaurus

Apatosaurus

Diplodocus

Mamenchisaurus wins in the neck division. Its neck was thirty-three feet long. See how it compared with other long-necked dinosaurs. A giraffe today has a neck more than six feet long.

Some dinosaurs had so many sharp teeth that they could chop up almost any plant. **Edmontosaurus** may have had a thousand teeth! As soon as one wore out, a new one grew in to take its place.

Watch out for **Tyrannosaurus**, forty feet long and weighing as much as six tons. This fierce meat-eating dinosaur had huge pointed teeth that curved backward, the better to get a grip on any prey. Each tooth had a zigzag edge—just like a steak knife.

Many plant-eating dinosaurs had sharp claws. They used them to grasp food and to fight off enemies.

Iguanodon had a special weapon—thumb spikes. It also had big curved claws on its toes and fingers. Iguanodon was able to walk on two legs or on all four.

A dinosaur, whatever its size, would not have made a cuddly pet. Almost all dinosaurs had knobby or scaly skin. It probably felt like the skin of reptiles today, only much more so!

No one knows what color dinosaurs were. Scientists used to think they were brown or dull green. Some experts today think that they may have been brightly colored, some kinds even spotted or striped.

Where did dinosaur babies come from?

Their mothers laid eggs with tough shells, just as crocodiles do today. They laid these eggs on land. Some dinosaurs dug shallow holes as nests.

Saurolophus

Some dinosaur eggs were oval. Others were longer, and still others were round. None of them was as big, compared to the size of a dinosaur, as you might think. A huge egg would have needed a very thick shell. The poor baby inside would never have been strong enough to poke its way out.

Protoceratops

The first dinosaur fossils were discovered only about one hundred and seventy years ago. Since then, dinosaur remains—like the sampling on the page opposite—have been found all over the world. The map below shows just some of the places where dinosaur fossils have been found.

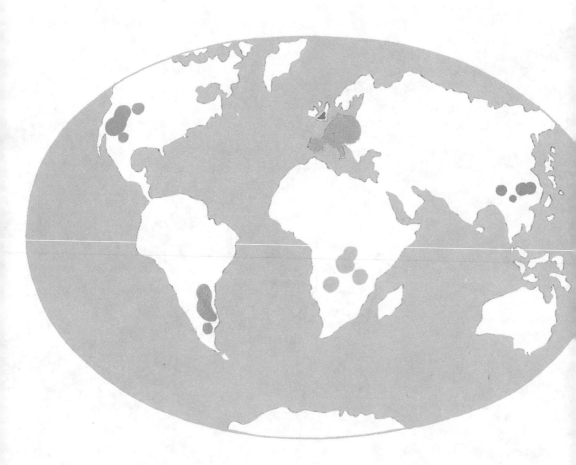

Plateosaurus skull
Found in Europe

Diplodocus leg bones
Found in England

**Brachiosaurus
jaws and teeth**
Found in North America

**Mamenchisaurus
hip bones**
Found in China

**Saltasaurus
foot bones**
Found in South America

**Anchisaurus
hand bones**
Found in Africa

Getting a dinosaur fossil out of soil or rock is a hard job. First, most of the rock must be hammered and chiseled away. Then the fossil must be covered with plaster to protect it.

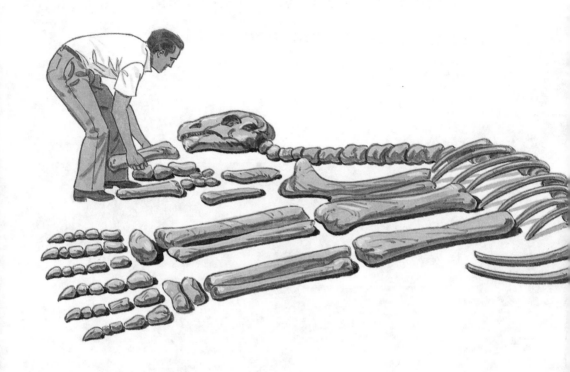

Next, it must be shipped to a museum or laboratory for study. Now the real work begins. Every bone must be carefully cleaned and examined. Perhaps a new piece will fit with other pieces from the same kind of dinosaur.

It is a little like working at a giant-sized jigsaw puzzle. If enough pieces of a dinosaur are found, a metal frame may be built to hold up its skeleton.

Sometimes, all that work produces a fantastic sight in a museum of natural history.

The dinosaur skeleton shown here is that
of **Apatosaurus**, once called Brontosaurus.

A part of the great mystery about the
disappearance of the dinosaurs 65 million years
ago is how other animals—land lizards, mammals,
turtles, frogs, sharks, and birds among others
living at the same time—managed to survive.
Some of the animals now living can be traced
back to the end of the Age of Dinosaurs.

Many people still think that the dinosaurs disappeared because they couldn't change as the world around them changed.

But scientists know that dinosaurs did keep changing. That is why the group lasted for about 150 million years!

Human beings have been living on earth for a much, much shorter time—less than 2 million years.

Here's an interesting question: Do you think human beings will survive on earth for as long as the dinosaurs did?

Here are some dinosaur names and how to say them.

Allosaurus	(al lo SAWR us)
Ankylosaurus	(an kyle o SAWR us)
Apatosaurus	(a pat o SAWR us)
Brachiosaurus	(brack e o SAWR us)
Camarasaurus	(kam ar ah SAWR us)
Coelurus	(see LURE us)
Compsognathus	(komp so NAY thus)
Edmontosaurus	(ed MONT o sawr us)
Hypsilophodon	(hip sih LOW fuh don)
Iguanodon	(i GWAN uh don)
Mamenchisaurus	(ma men ki SAWR us)
Parasaurolophus	(par uh sawr ALL uff us)
Plateosaurus	(plat e o SAWR us)
Saltasaurus	(SALT uh sawr us)
Scutellosaurus	(skoo tell o SAWR us)
Staurikosaurus	(stawr ik o SAWR us)
Stegosaurus	(steg o SAWR us)
Stenonychosaurus	(sten on IK uh sawr us)
Triceratops	(try SER a tops)
Tyrannosaurus	(tye ran o SAWR us)